Wake Up, Grizzly!

By Wolfgang Bittner · Illustrated by Gustavo Rosemffet

Translated by J. Alison James

North-South Books / New York / London

One Sunday morning when Toby woke
up, he heard a bear rumbling and growling
somewhere in the house—HUMPF . . . HUMPF . . .
GRRUMM.

He crept out of bed and tiptoed down
the hall.

Mother was brushing her teeth. No bear there.

The sound got louder: HUMPF . . . HUMPF . . . GRRUMM. It was coming from his parents' room. Toby slowly opened the door.

HUMPF . . . HUMPF . . . GRRUMM!
There was the bear! A big brown
bear, right in the middle of the bed!
Bravely Toby jumped on the bed to
chase the bear away. But it wasn't a
bear after all. It was Dad, snoring!
Dad liked to sleep late on Sundays.

It was raining outside and Toby's
toes were cold. The bed looked cozy
and warm. Toby started to climb
inside.

GRROWLLL!

"I thought you were a bear," said Toby. "You were snoring so loud."

"I am a bear," laughed Dad. "I'm Big Grizzly—and I'm going to eat you up!"

"Eek!" cried Toby. "Don't bite me!"

"I would never bite you," Dad said as he settled comfortably on his back and swooped Toby high in the air. "You are Little Grizzly."

"Oh," said Toby. "Where do we live?"

"Here in our bear den," said Dad, lifting up the quilt.

Toby looked inside. Wow, was it dark!

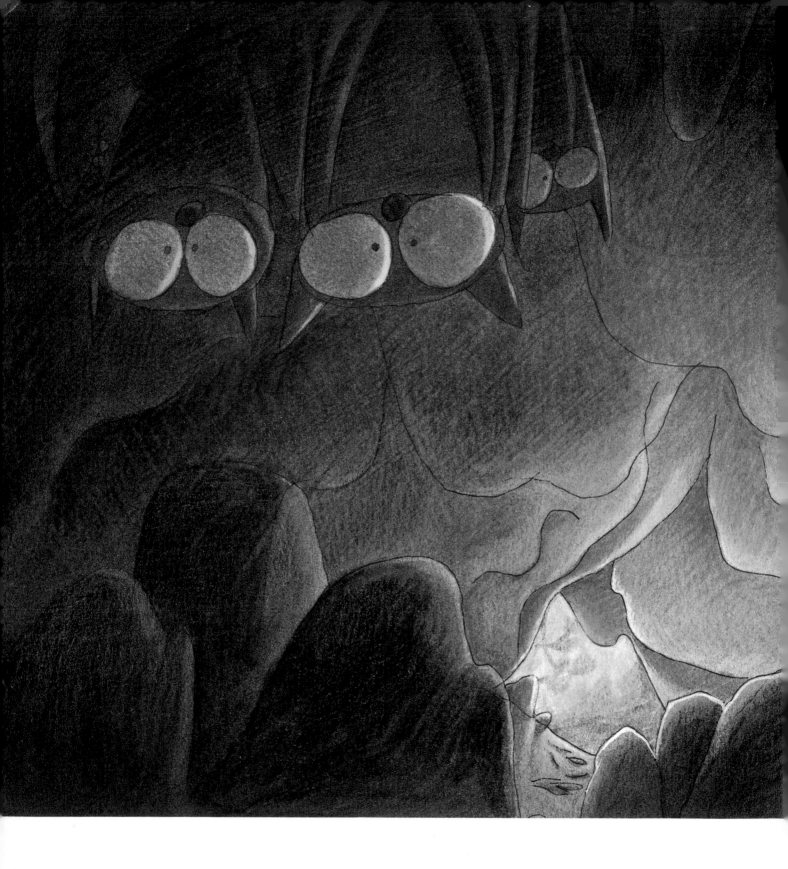

The den was big enough for a big
bear and a small bear.

Just a little light came in from the
mouth of the cave.

"What do bears eat?" asked Little
Grizzly.

Big Grizzly pondered for a minute.
Then he answered: "Gummy Bears,
of course."

"Great!" said Little Grizzly. "I think
I still have a few left in my pocket.
They're only a little sticky."

"That doesn't matter," Big Grizzly
replied. "Hand one over. I'm hungry
as a bear! Mmm, delicious!"

CRACK! CRACK! came a sound from outside their cave.

"Hunters!" whispered Big Grizzly. "We have to lie very still and quiet, so they don't find us."

They lay there for a while, very quietly. Then suddenly Big Grizzly began to snore. He was asleep! How could he fall asleep at a time like this?

The hunters were searching for the mouth of the bears' cave. They were getting very close!

Dad was still snoring. He sounded like a chainsaw cutting through a tree.

Toby put his hand over Dad's mouth so the hunters wouldn't hear him. It didn't help. He pinched Dad's nose shut. That worked.

Dad sneezed and spluttered.

"Shhh!" whispered Toby. "Hunters!"

"It's just the radiator banging," said Dad. "There's nothing to be afraid of."

All was quiet. Then . . .

Creech . . . screeck!

What was that? Maybe it was
a tiger trying to get in.

Toby was scared.

"It's just a branch scratching
the windowpane," said Dad.
"Listen carefully."

All was quiet. Then . . .

TAP! What was that? TAP . . . TAP! Something was walking on top of their cave. Even Big Grizzly was afraid this time.

All at once they saw a paw with outstretched claws reaching in to get them.

It really was a tiger! She crawled inside and purred loudly.

"She's not allowed on the bed," said Dad. "But we'll make an exception."

The tiger got a Gummy Bear too. Then she curled up between the grizzly bears. It was warm and quiet and dark in their den. The bears gently rumbled and the tiger purred.

Suddenly the cave was ripped apart. The bears woke up from their long winter's sleep. The sun was shining, and something smelled good.

"Get up, you lazybones," cried Mother with a laugh. "Waffles for breakfast!"

"I want honey on mine," said Dad. "Grizzly bears just love honey."

"Me too!" said Toby, and he scampered out of bed.